PILOT MAX'S
BETRAYAL

PILOT MAX'S BETRAYAL

AuthorHouse™
1663 Liberty Drive
Bloomington, IN 47403
www.authorhouse.com
Phone: 833-262-8899

Because of the dynamic nature of the Internet, any web addresses or links contained in this book may have changed
since publication and may no longer be valid. The views expressed in this work are solely those of the author and do
not necessarily reflect the views of the publisher, and the publisher hereby disclaims any responsibility for them.

Any people depicted in stock imagery provided by Getty Images are models,
and such images are being used for illustrative purposes only.
Certain stock imagery © Getty Images.

This book is printed on acid-free paper.

ISBN: 978-1-6655-6572-1 (sc)
ISBN: 978-1-6655-6573-8 (e)

Print information available on the last page.

Published by AuthorHouse 07/19/2022

authorHOUSE®

Janine talks to the gals at work to find out exactly what is going on with Pilot Max.

Janine surmised she may have been more privy to Max's updated information from the gals but to no avail. She realizes she must dig deeper.

ORIGINAL

Janine felt sick to her stomach all day. Her involvement with Pilot Max's did something to her. She must see a doctor.

SG♥
ORIGINAL

MEANWHILE...
THE BEARER OF
NECESSARY NEWS

Frandley
Airport

COLD AND WARM AT THE SAME TIME.

Flight attendant Janine needs your help. She's pregnant, Pilot Max is a long way away, he doesn't care.

Freedom.. I'm already ready. Hook me up.

Good to see you by the way.

SG ♥ ORIGINAL

PAGE 11

PILOT MAX'S BETRAYAL

LET WILD BE WILD...

It's like this… if you're enchanted by a player like Pilot Max appreciate him from afar.

He won't change. Let him be.

It's almost as if he is made to be this way.

All the agonizing over his disloyalty will go nowhere.

And your intent on perpetuating a future fantasy with him will result in a broken heart,

What is… is.

You made your decision. If your decision resulted in a baby with a run around let it build you instead of culminating into an endless "surprise." No need to waste any more of your priceless time.

You could look at Pilot Max as a gift … or a lesson.

And question the answer:

"How will you utilize the lesson of Pilot Max?"

Sean Gentile
The Questor, 2022

TO BE CONTINUED

Printed in the United States
by Baker & Taylor Publisher Services